A 4D BOOK

ADVENTURES IN MAKERSPACE

A CODING MISSION

WRITTEN BY
SHANNON MCCLINTOCK MILLER
AND
BLAKE HOENA

ILLUSTRATED BY
ALAN BROWN

STONE ARCH BOOKS
a capstone imprint

capstone®

www.mycapstone.com

A Coding Mission is published by Stone Arch Books,
a Capstone imprint
1710 Roe Crest Drive, North Mankato, Minnesota 56003
www.mycapstonepub.com

Library of Congress Cataloging-in-Publication Data is available on the
Library of Congress website.

ISBN: 978-1-4965-7743-6 (hardcover)
ISBN: 978-1-4965-7747-4 (paperback)
ISBN: 978-1-4965-7751-1 (eBook PDF)

Book design and art direction: Mighty Media
Editorial direction: Kellie M. Hultgren
Music direction: Elizabeth Draper
Music written and produced by Mark Mallman

Printed and bound in the United States of America.
082018   000044

CONTENTS

Download the Capstone 4D app!

- Ask an adult to download the Capstone 4D app.
- Scan the cover and stars inside the book for additional content.

When you scan a spread, you'll find fun extra stuff to go with this book! You can also find these things on the web at www.capstone4D.com using the password: code.77436

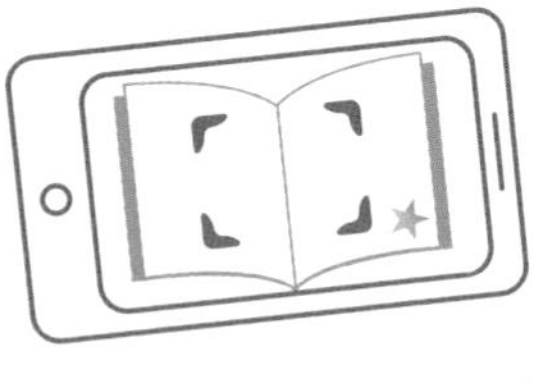

MEET THE SPECIALIST

ABILITIES:
speed reader, tech titan,
foreign language master,
traveler through literature
and history

MS. GILLIAN
TEACHER-LIBRARIAN

MEET THE STUDENTS

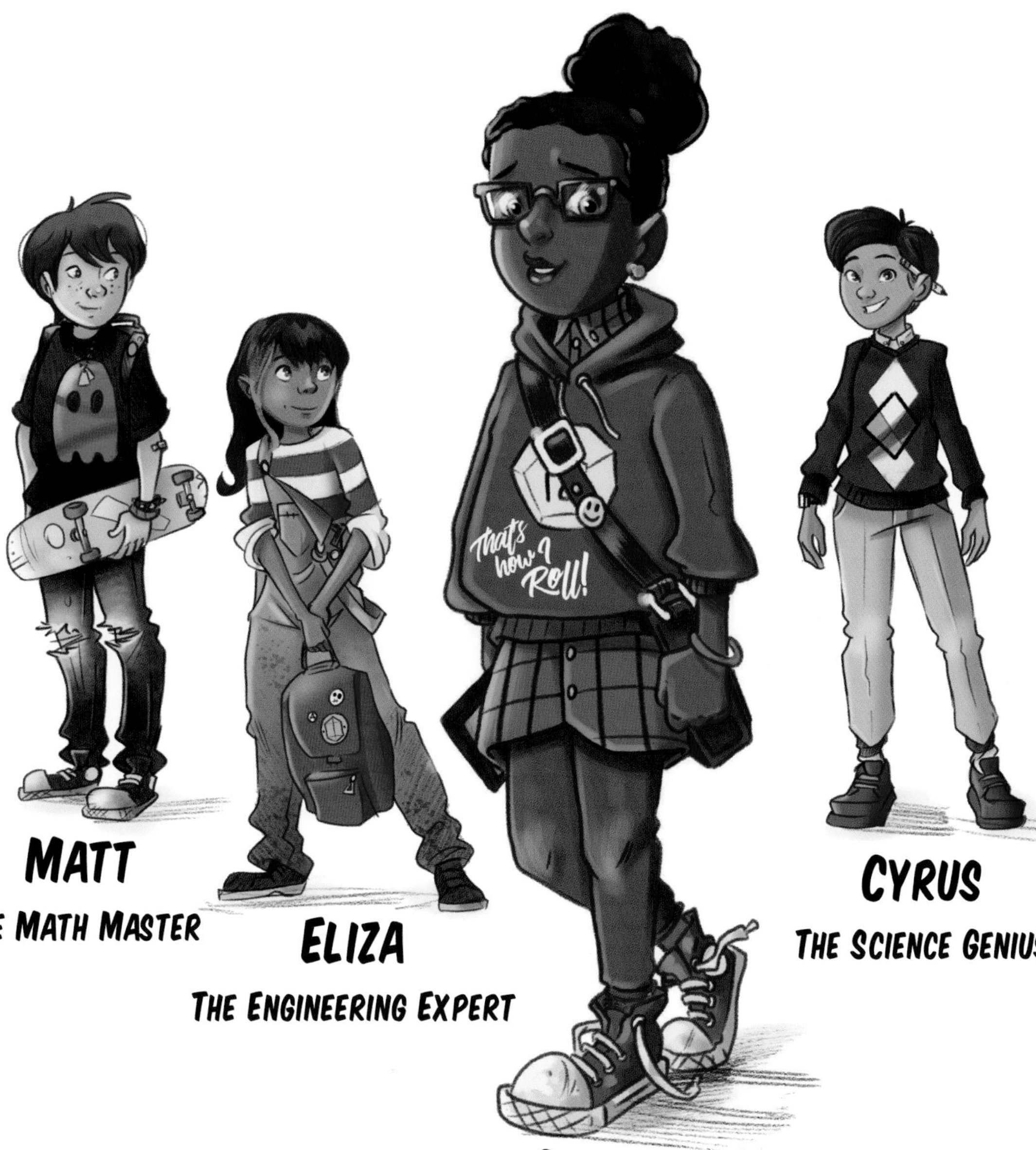
That's how I Roll!

MATT
THE MATH MASTER

ELIZA
THE ENGINEERING EXPERT

CYRUS
THE SCIENCE GENIUS

CODIE
THE CODING WHIZ

THE LABYRINTH

FOR CODIE AND HER FRIENDS, IT IS ANOTHER BUSY DAY AT EMERSON ELEMENTARY. THEY ARE ON THEIR WAY TO ONE OF THE MOST EXCITING PLACES IN SCHOOL. IT IS AN AREA OF THE LIBRARY THAT MS. GILLIAN CALLS THE MAKERSPACE.

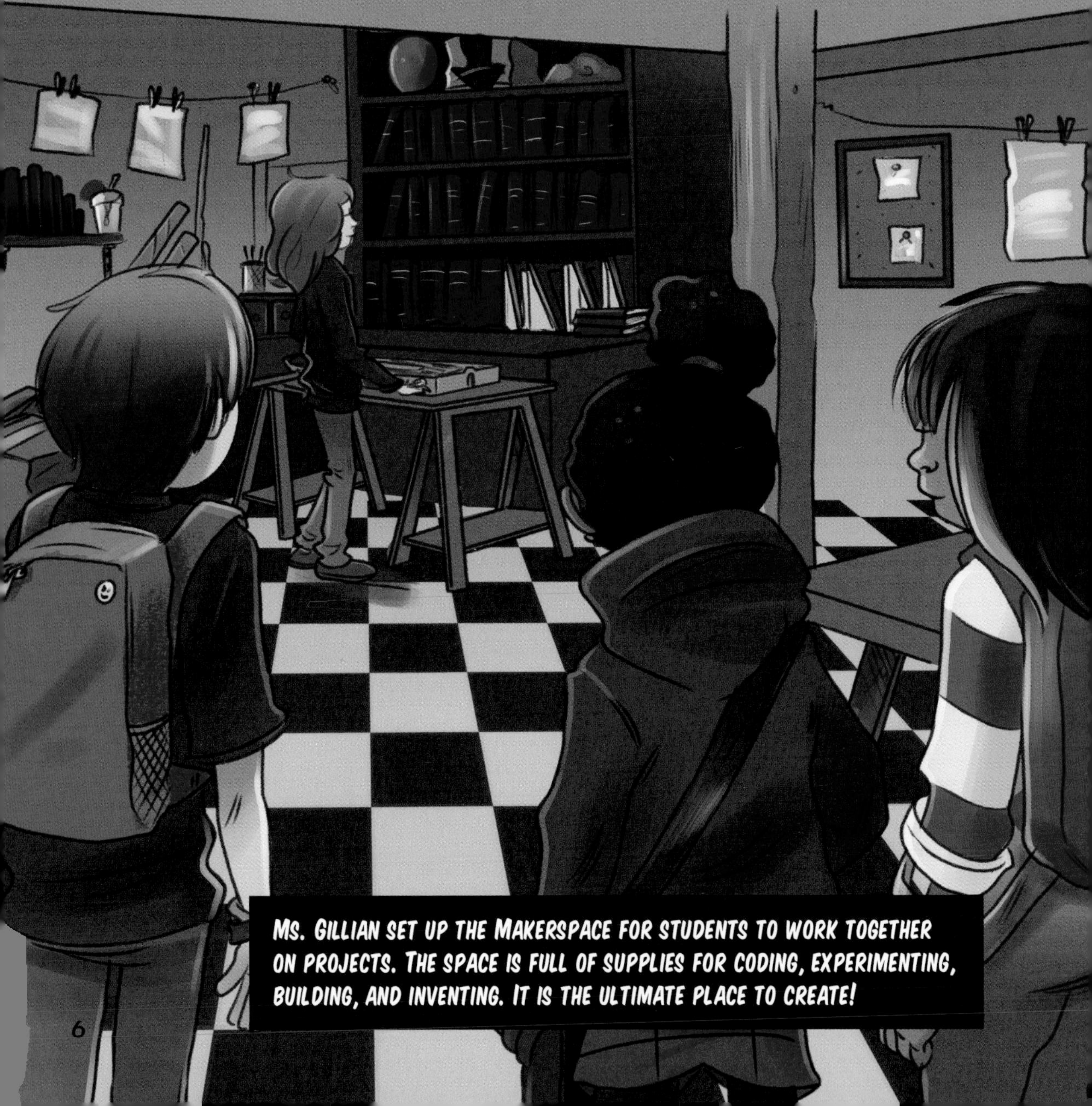
MS. GILLIAN SET UP THE MAKERSPACE FOR STUDENTS TO WORK TOGETHER ON PROJECTS. THE SPACE IS FULL OF SUPPLIES FOR CODING, EXPERIMENTING, BUILDING, AND INVENTING. IT IS THE ULTIMATE PLACE TO CREATE!

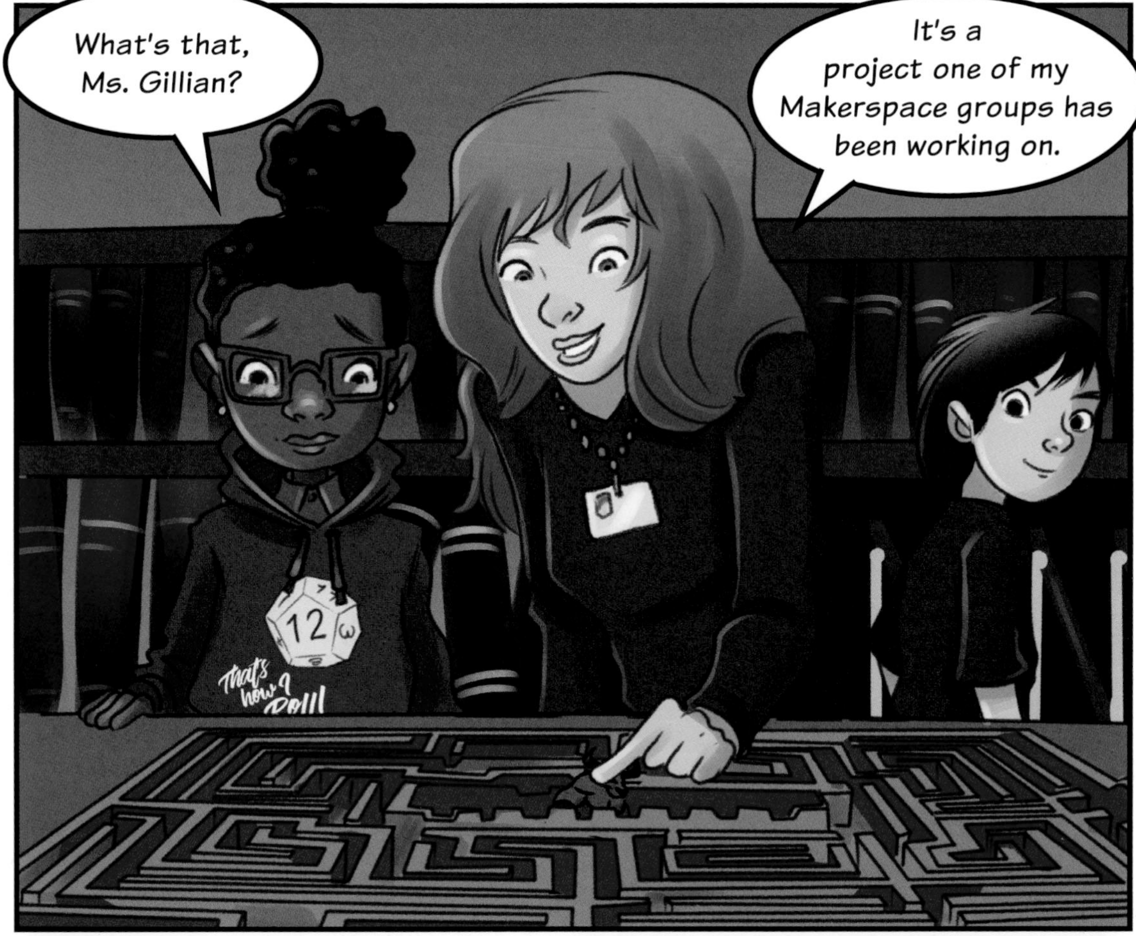
What's that, Ms. Gillian?
It's a project one of my Makerspace groups has been working on.

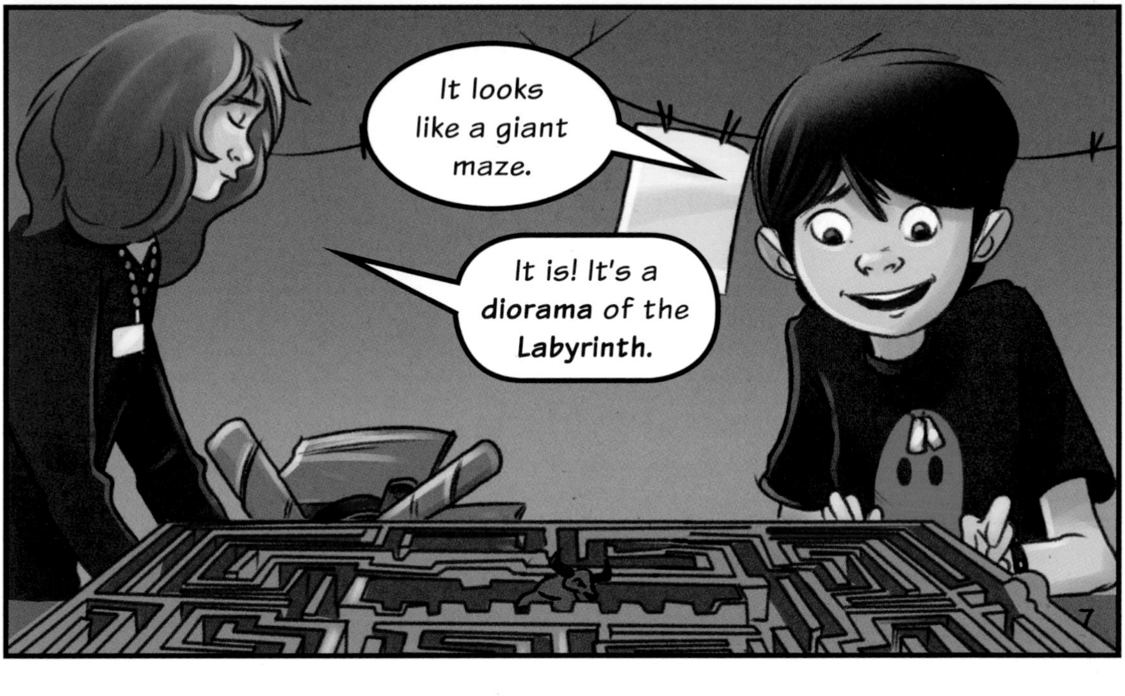
It looks like a giant maze.
It is! It's a **diorama** of the **Labyrinth**.

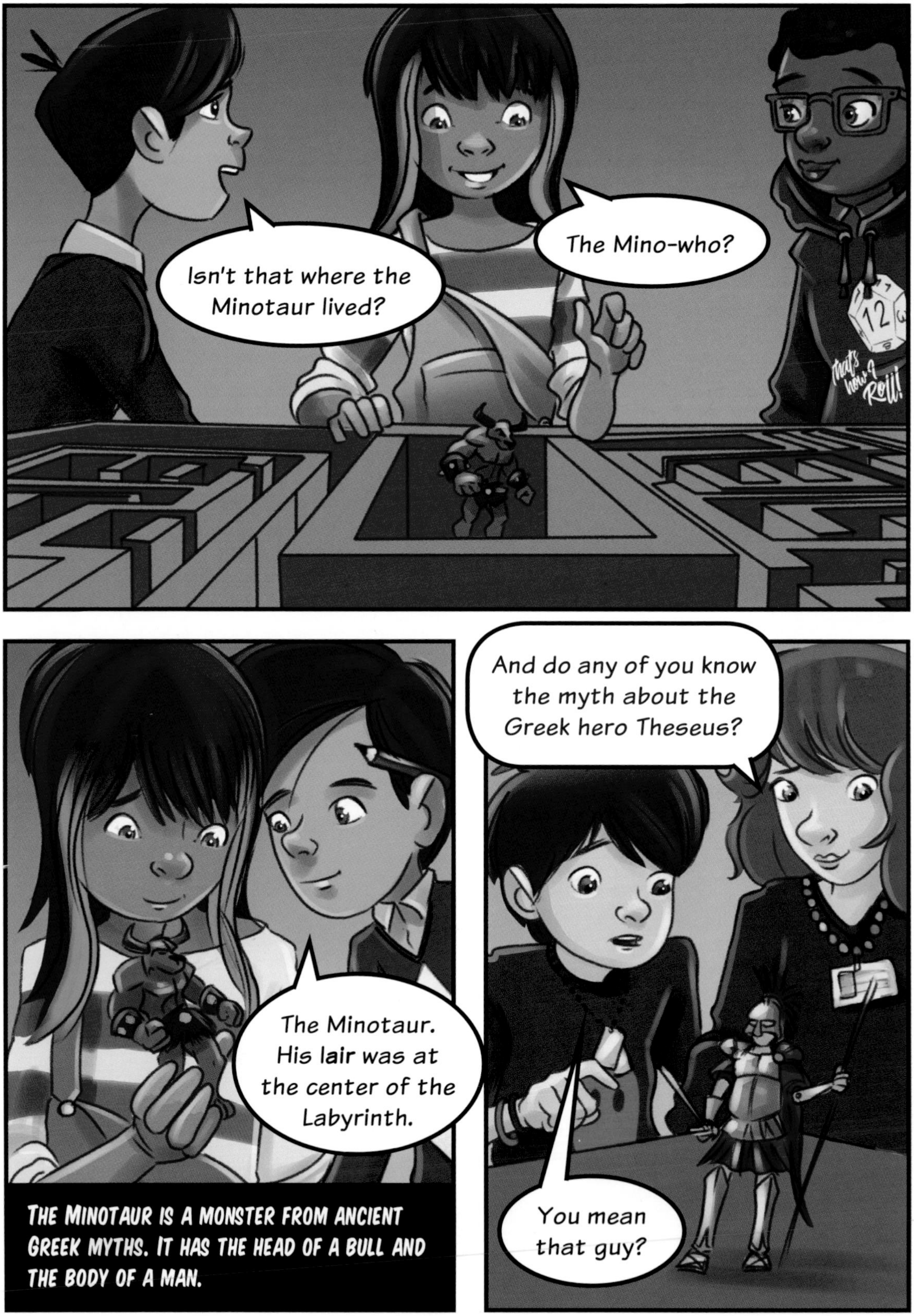
Isn't that where the Minotaur lived?
The Mino-who?
The Minotaur. His lair was at the center of the Labyrinth.
THE MINOTAUR IS A MONSTER FROM ANCIENT GREEK MYTHS. IT HAS THE HEAD OF A BULL AND THE BODY OF A MAN.
And do any of you know the myth about the Greek hero Theseus?
You mean that guy?

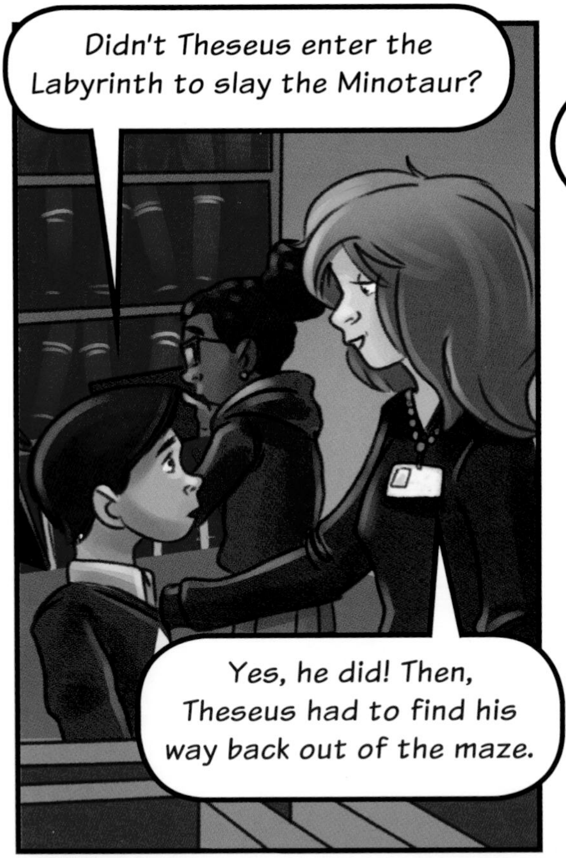
Didn't Theseus enter the Labyrinth to slay the Minotaur?
Yes, he did! Then, Theseus had to find his way back out of the maze.

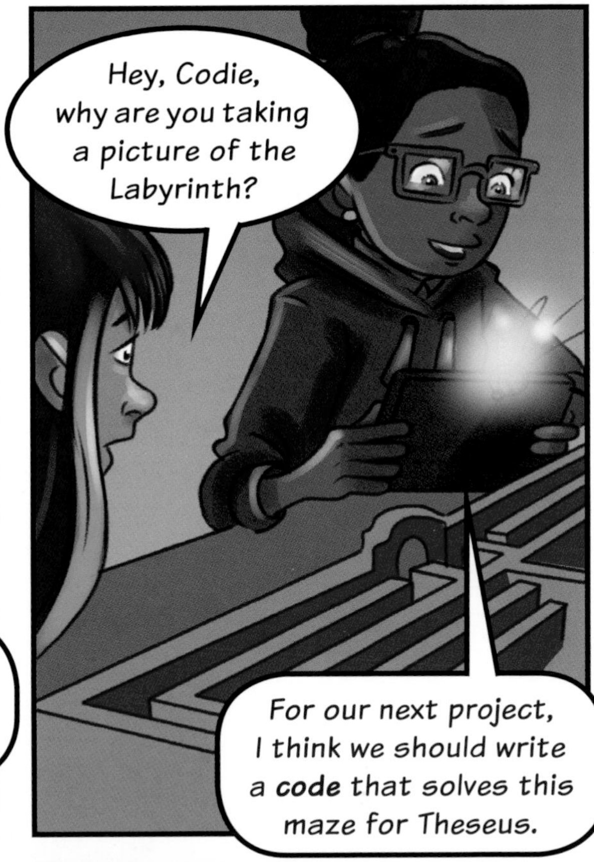
Hey, Codie, why are you taking a picture of the Labyrinth?
For our next project, I think we should write a **code** that solves this maze for Theseus.

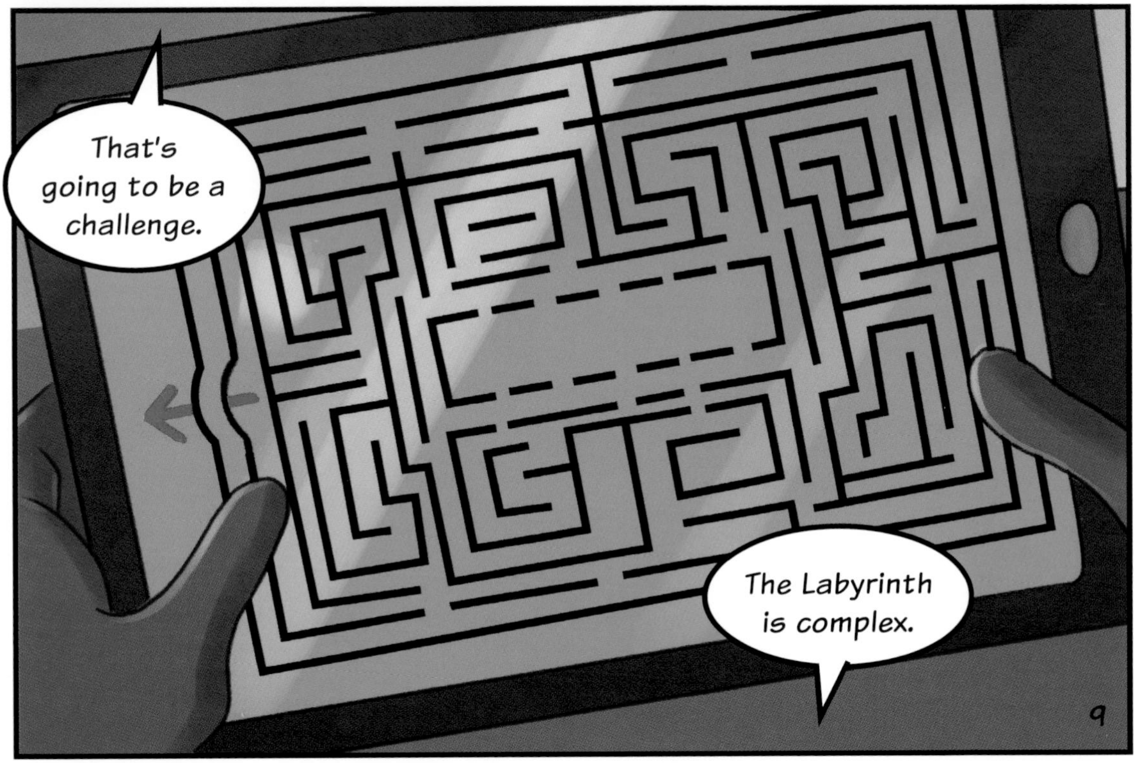
That's going to be a challenge.
The Labyrinth is complex.

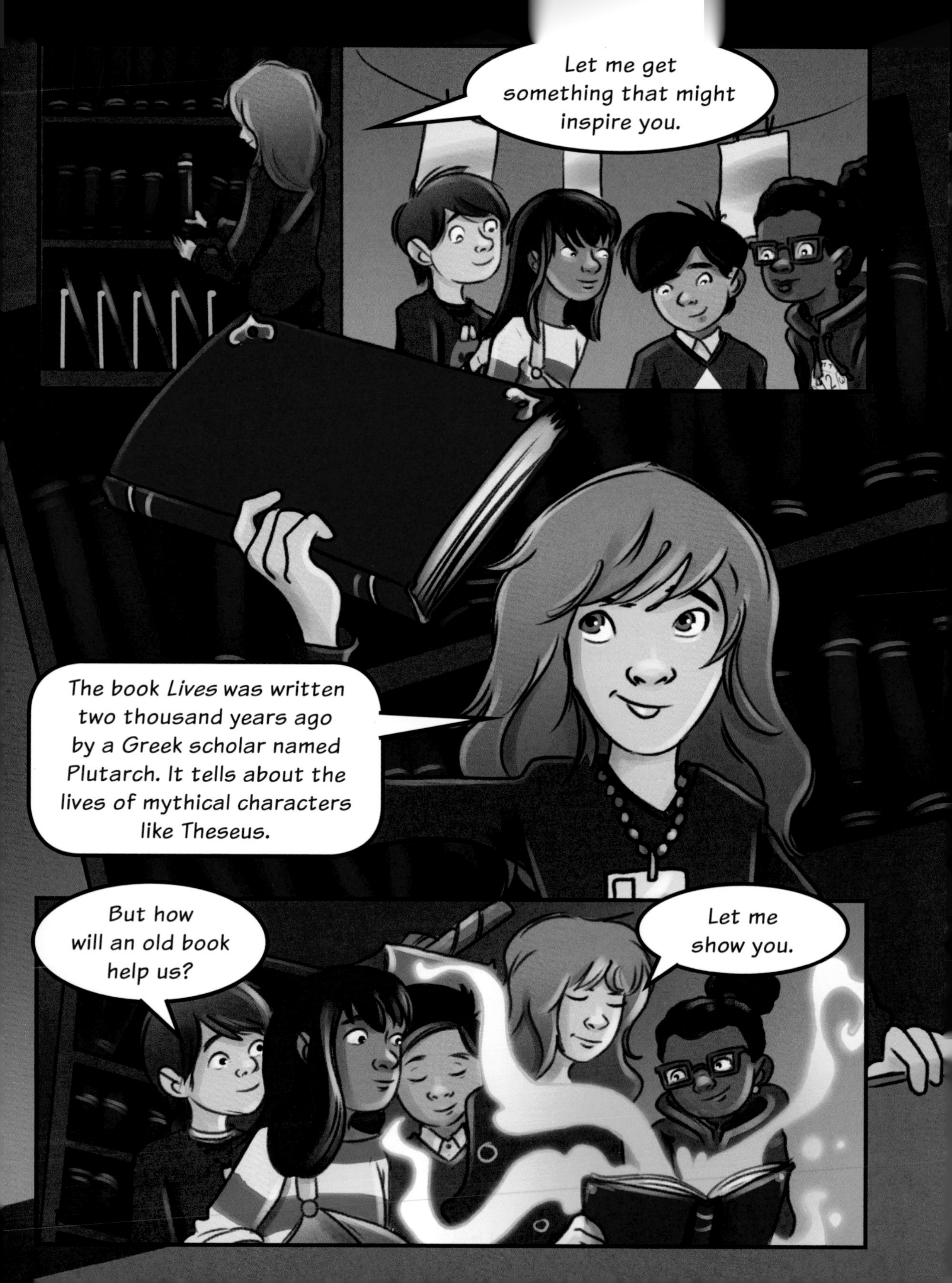
Let me get something that might inspire you.
The book *Lives* was written two thousand years ago by a Greek scholar named Plutarch. It tells about the lives of mythical characters like Theseus.
But how will an old book help us?
Let me show you.

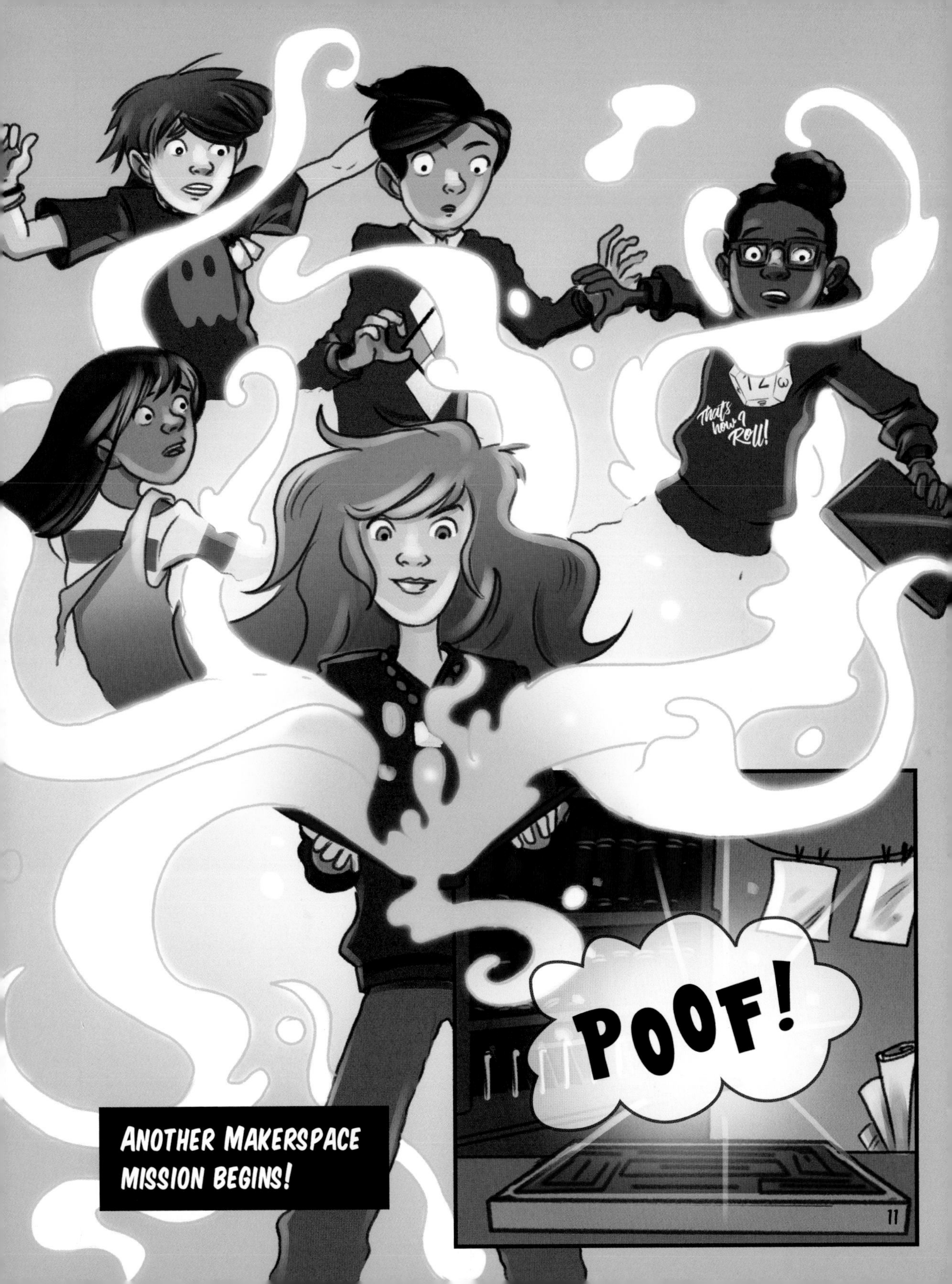
That's how I Roll!
POOF!
ANOTHER MAKERSPACE MISSION BEGINS!

THE MINOTAUR'S LAIR

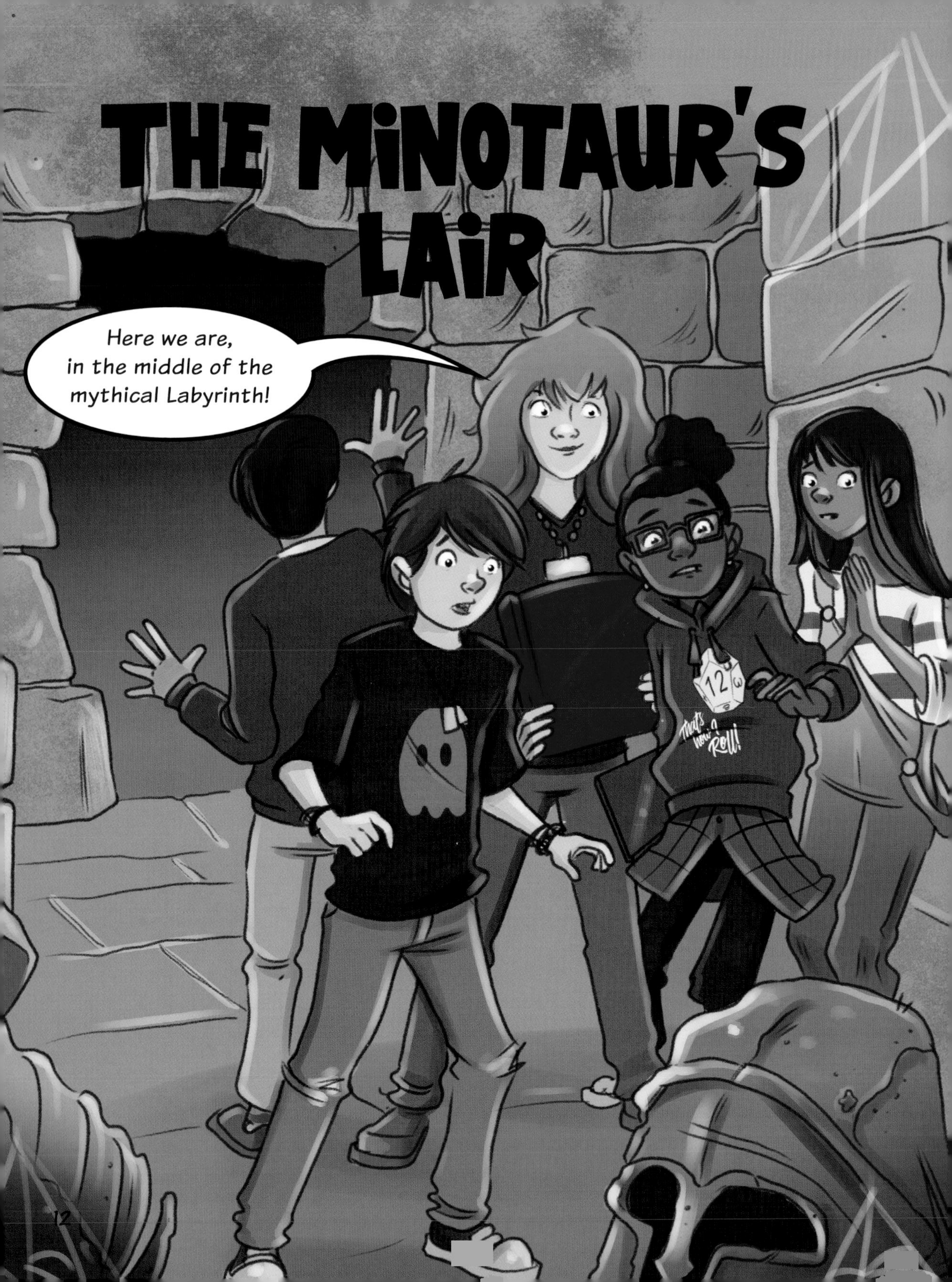
Here we are, in the middle of the mythical Labyrinth!

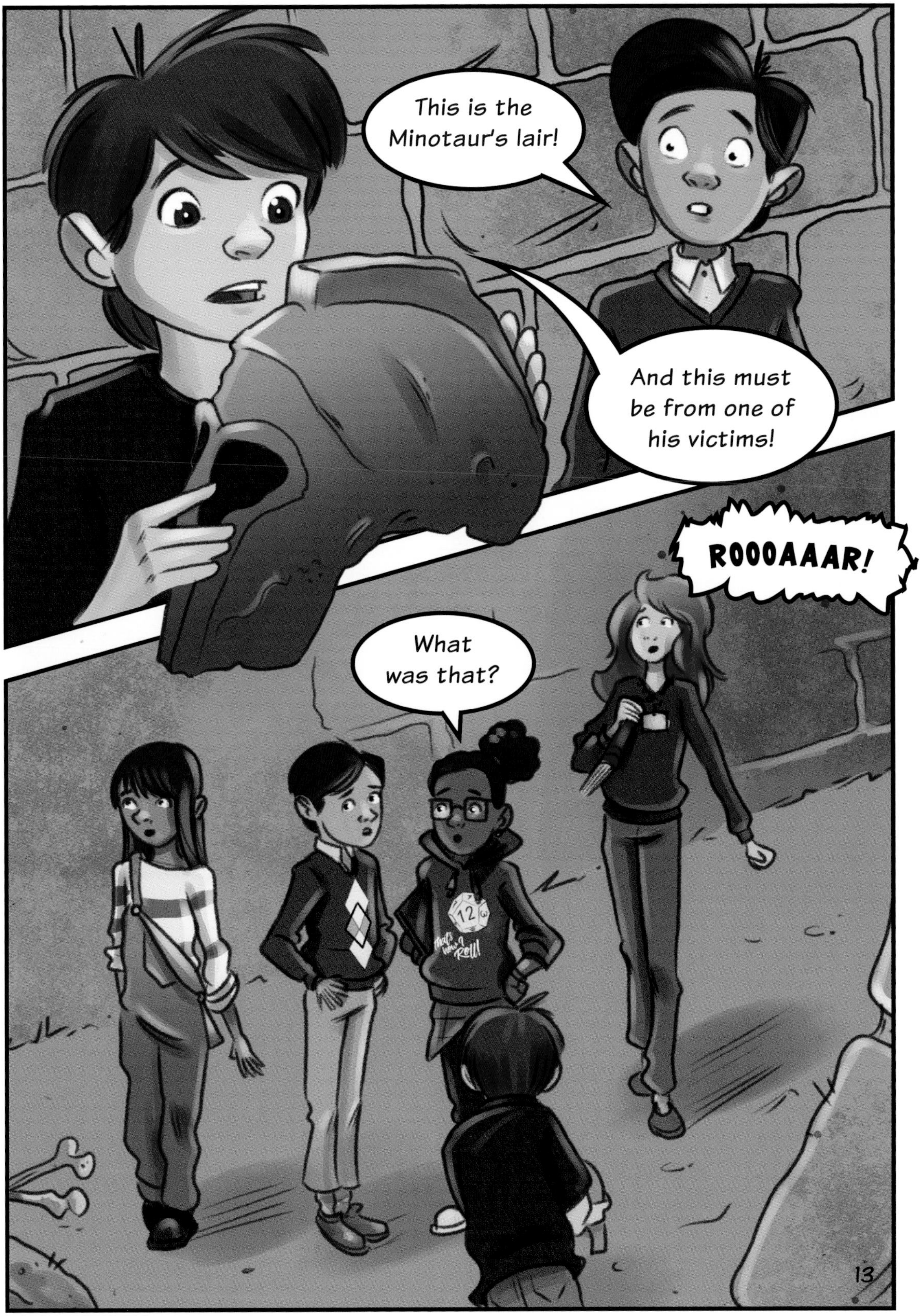
This is the Minotaur's lair!
And this must be from one of his victims!
ROOOAAAR!
What was that?

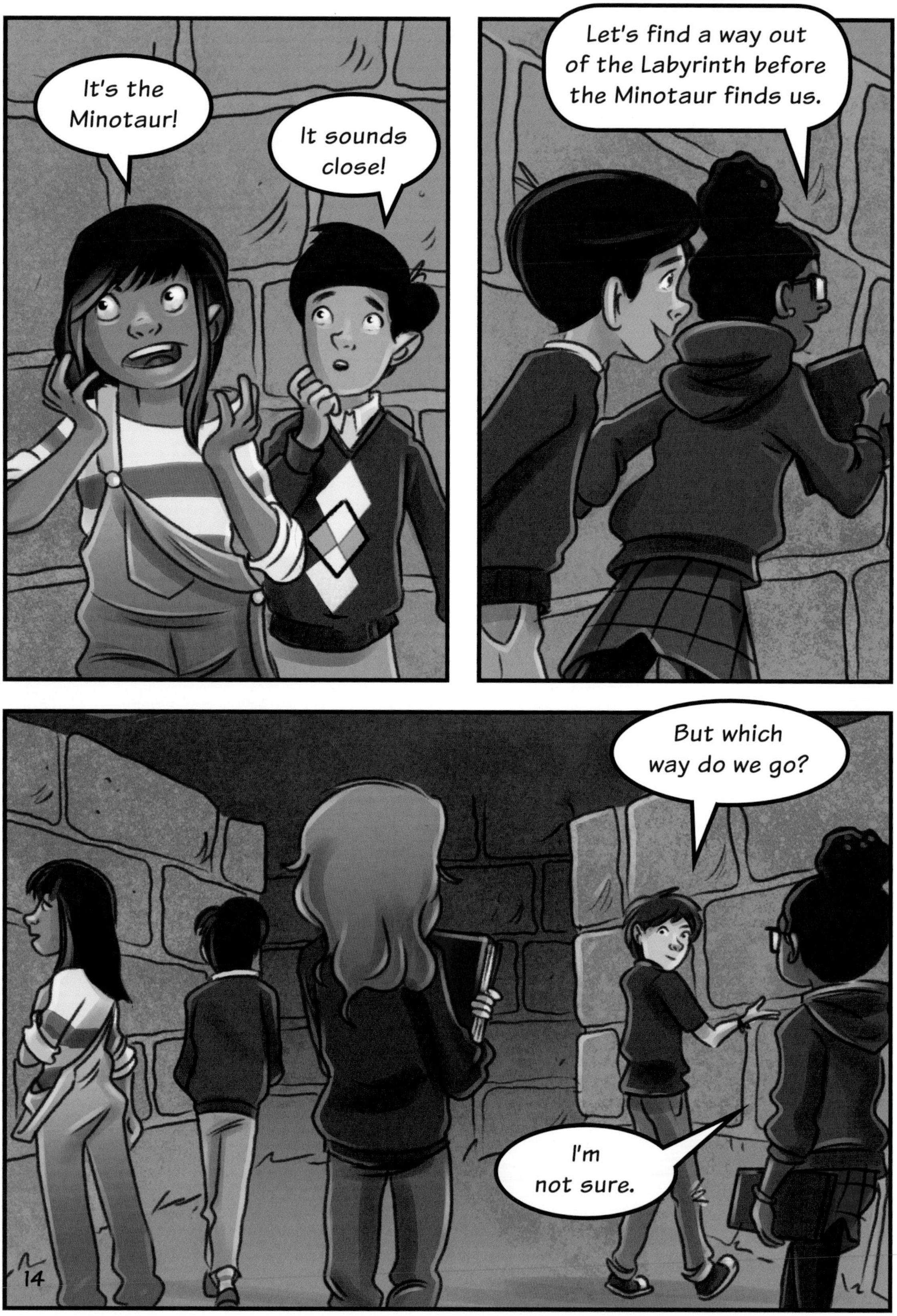
It's the Minotaur!
It sounds close!
Let's find a way out of the Labyrinth before the Minotaur finds us.
But which way do we go?
I'm not sure.

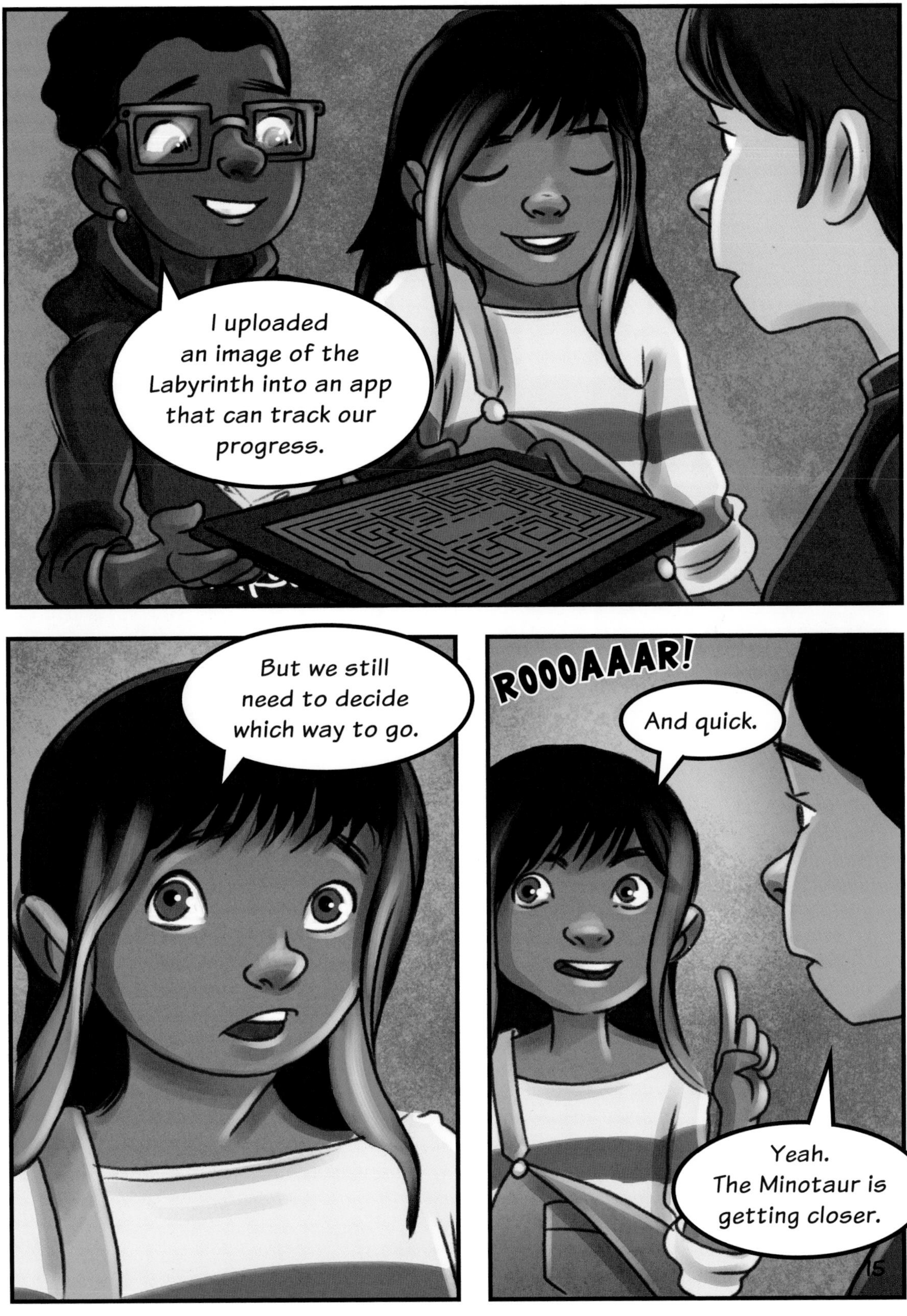
I uploaded an image of the Labyrinth into an app that can track our progress.
But we still need to decide which way to go.
ROOOAAAR!
And quick.
Yeah. The Minotaur is getting closer.

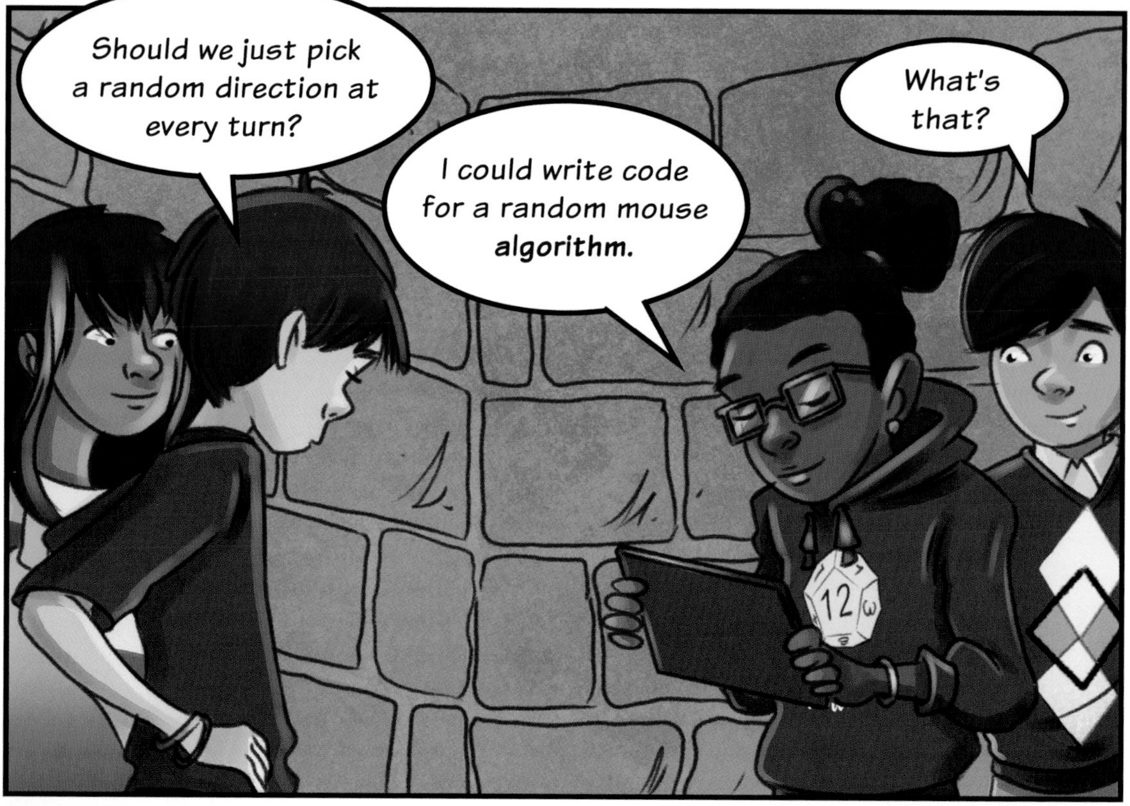
Should we just pick a random direction at every turn?
I could write code for a random mouse **algorithm.**
What's that?

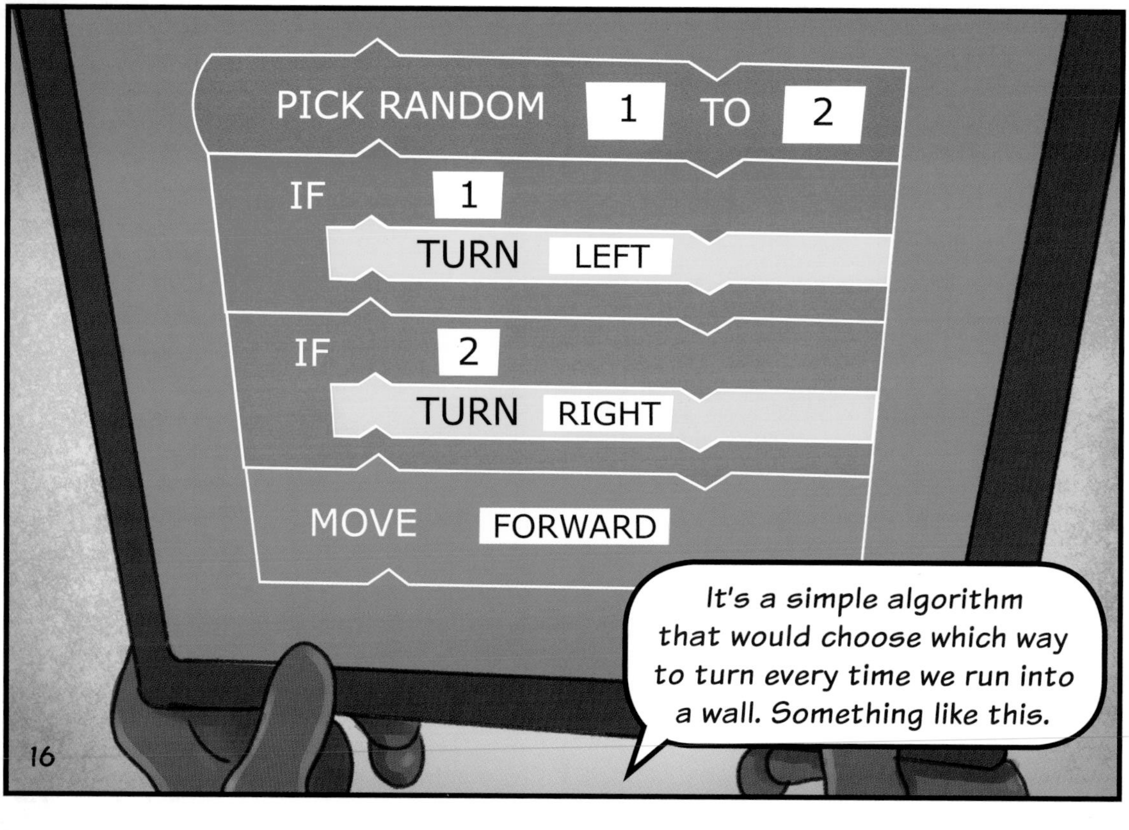
PICK RANDOM 1 TO 2
IF 1
TURN LEFT
IF 2
TURN RIGHT
MOVE FORWARD
It's a simple algorithm that would choose which way to turn every time we run into a wall. Something like this.

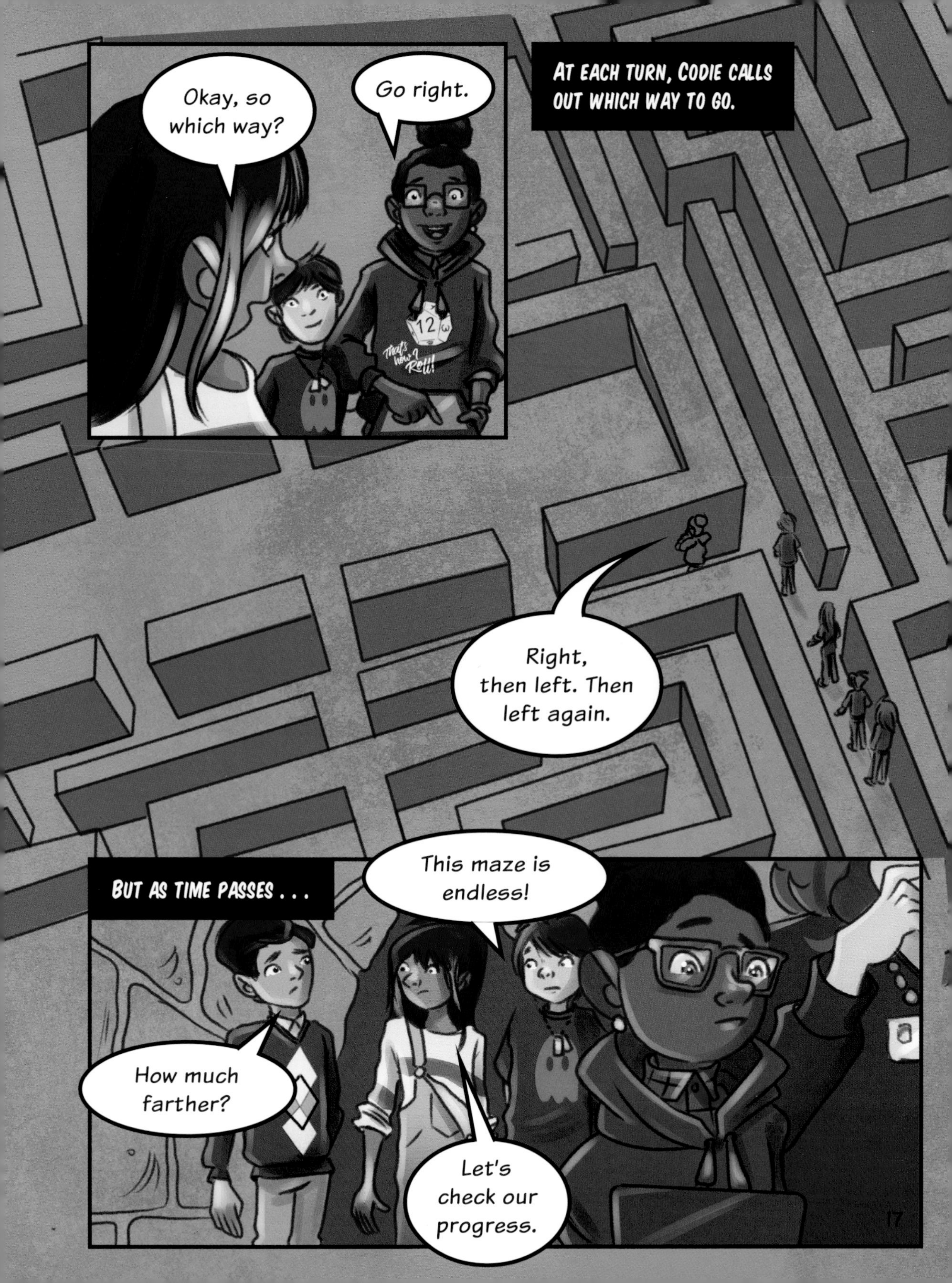
Okay, so which way?
Go right.
At each turn, Codie calls out which way to go.
12
That's how I Roll!
Right, then left. Then left again.
But as time passes . . .
This maze is endless!
How much farther?
Let's check our progress.

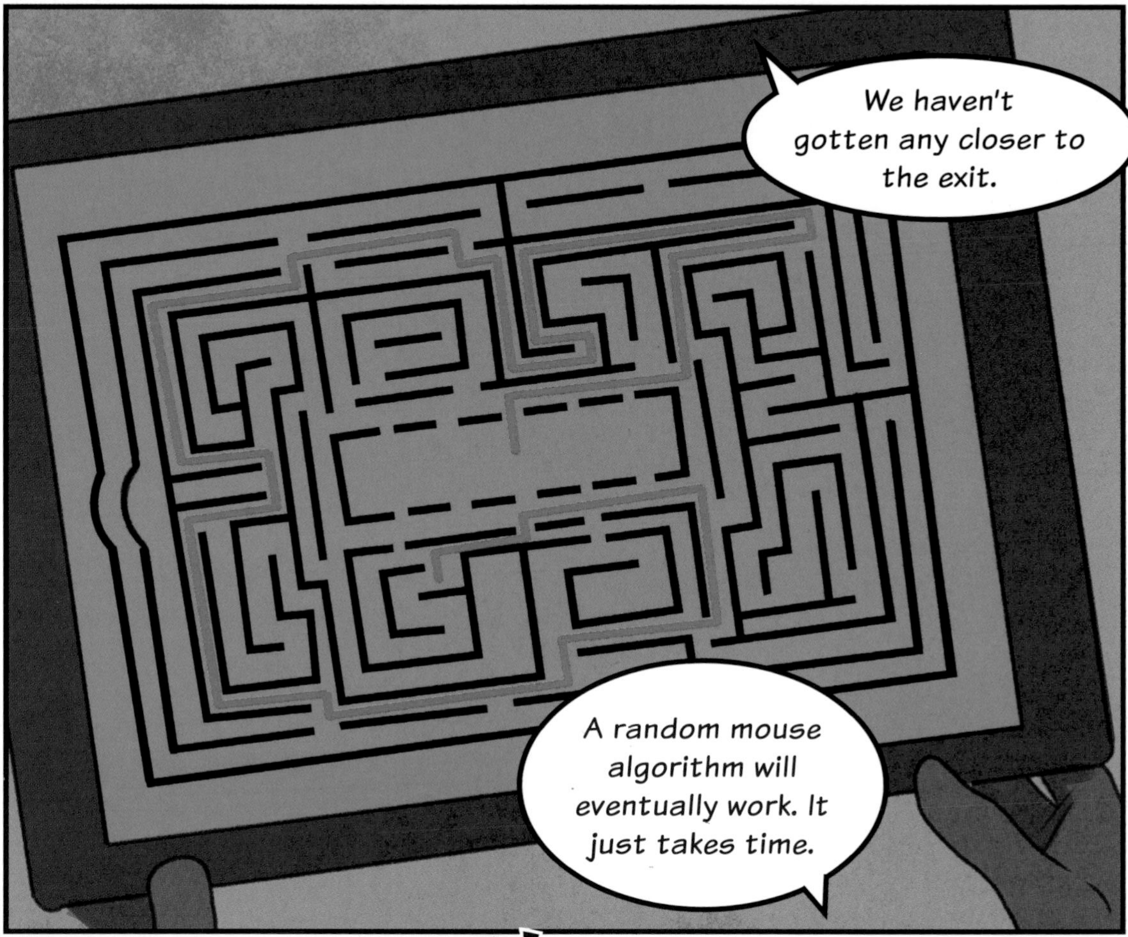
We haven't gotten any closer to the exit.
A random mouse algorithm will eventually work. It just takes time.

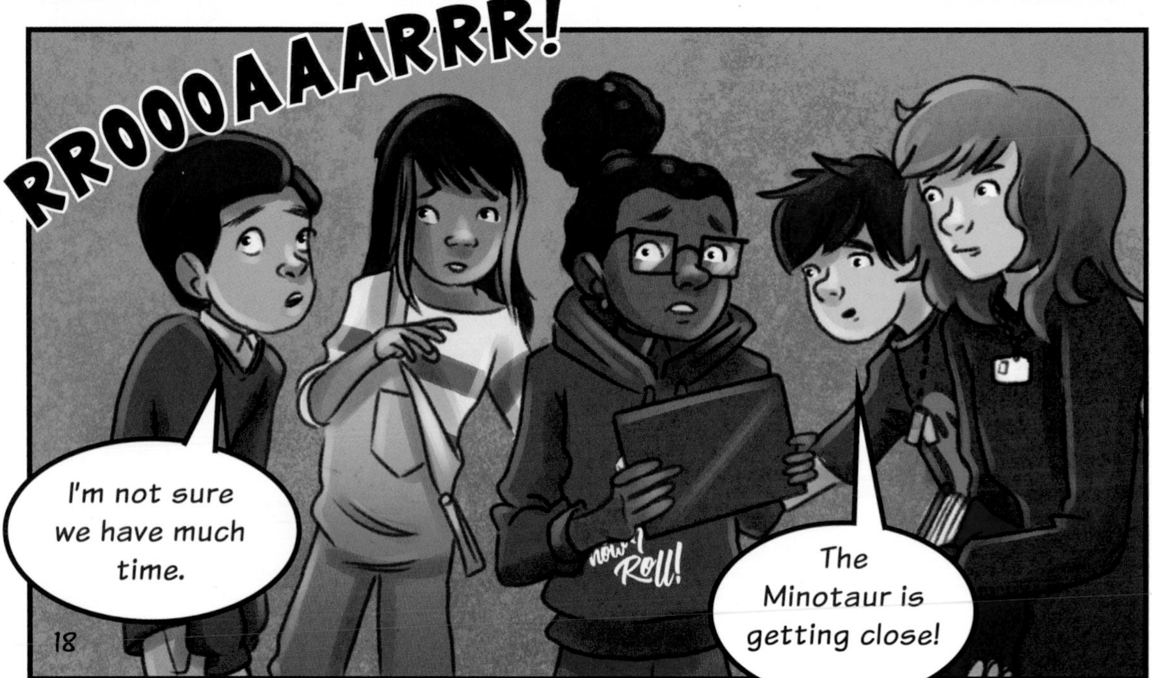
RROOOAAARRR!
I'm not sure we have much time.
The Minotaur is getting close!

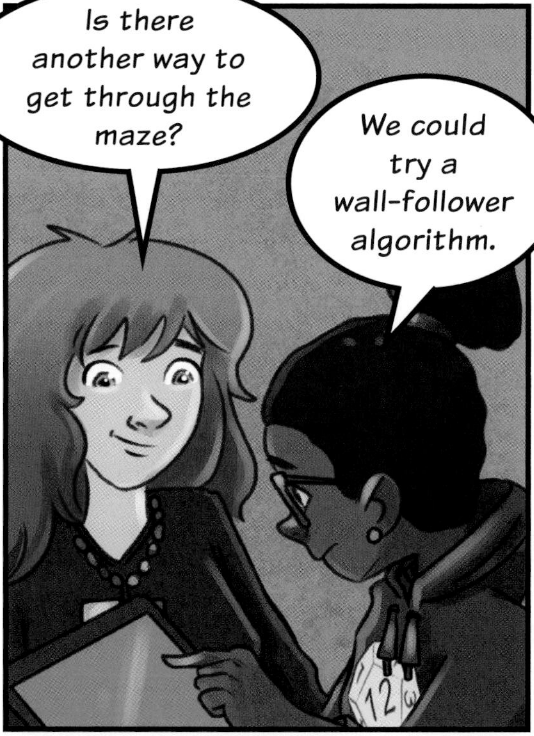
Is there another way to get through the maze?
We could try a wall-follower algorithm.

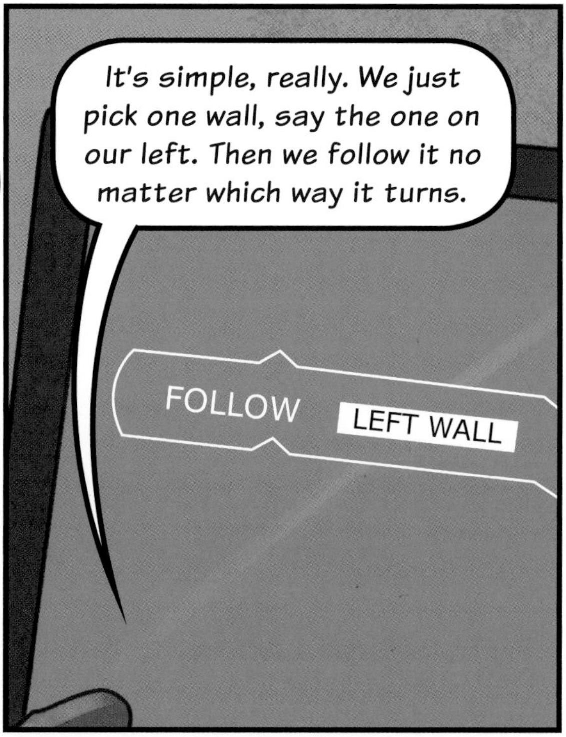
It's simple, really. We just pick one wall, say the one on our left. Then we follow it no matter which way it turns.
FOLLOW
LEFT WALL

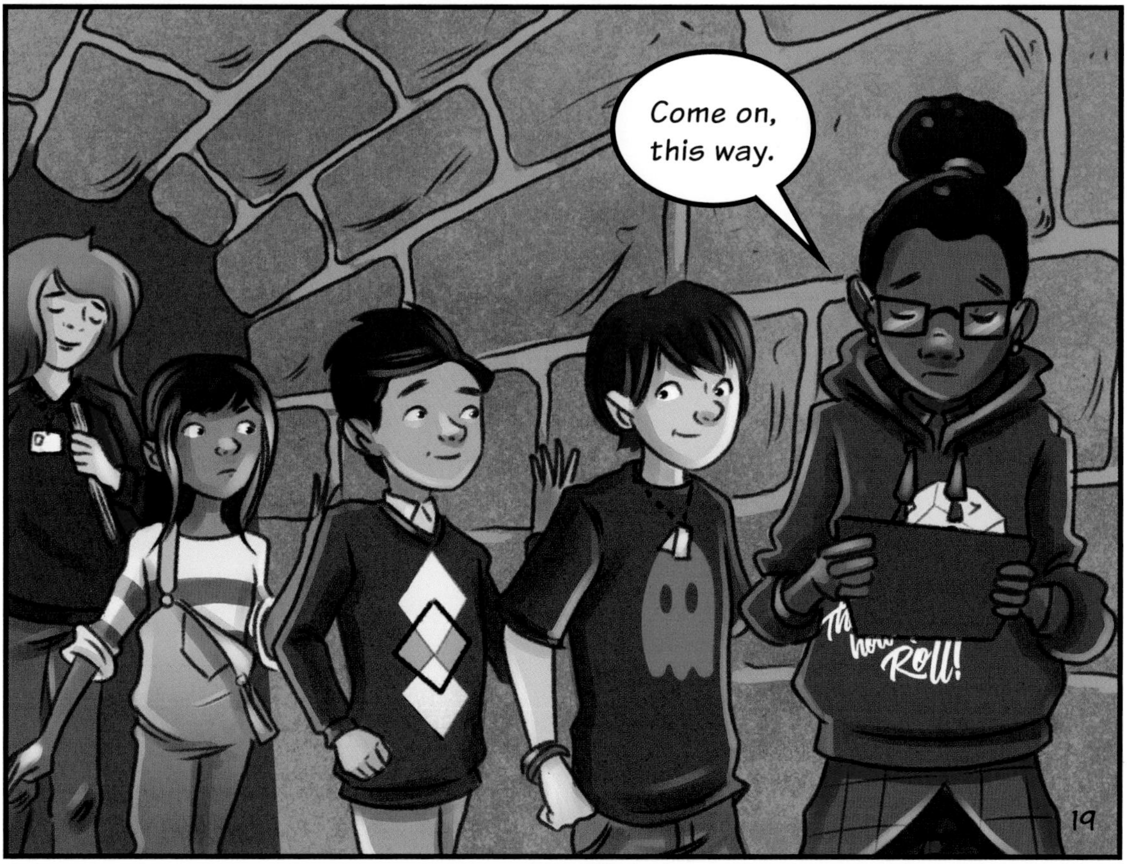
Come on, this way.

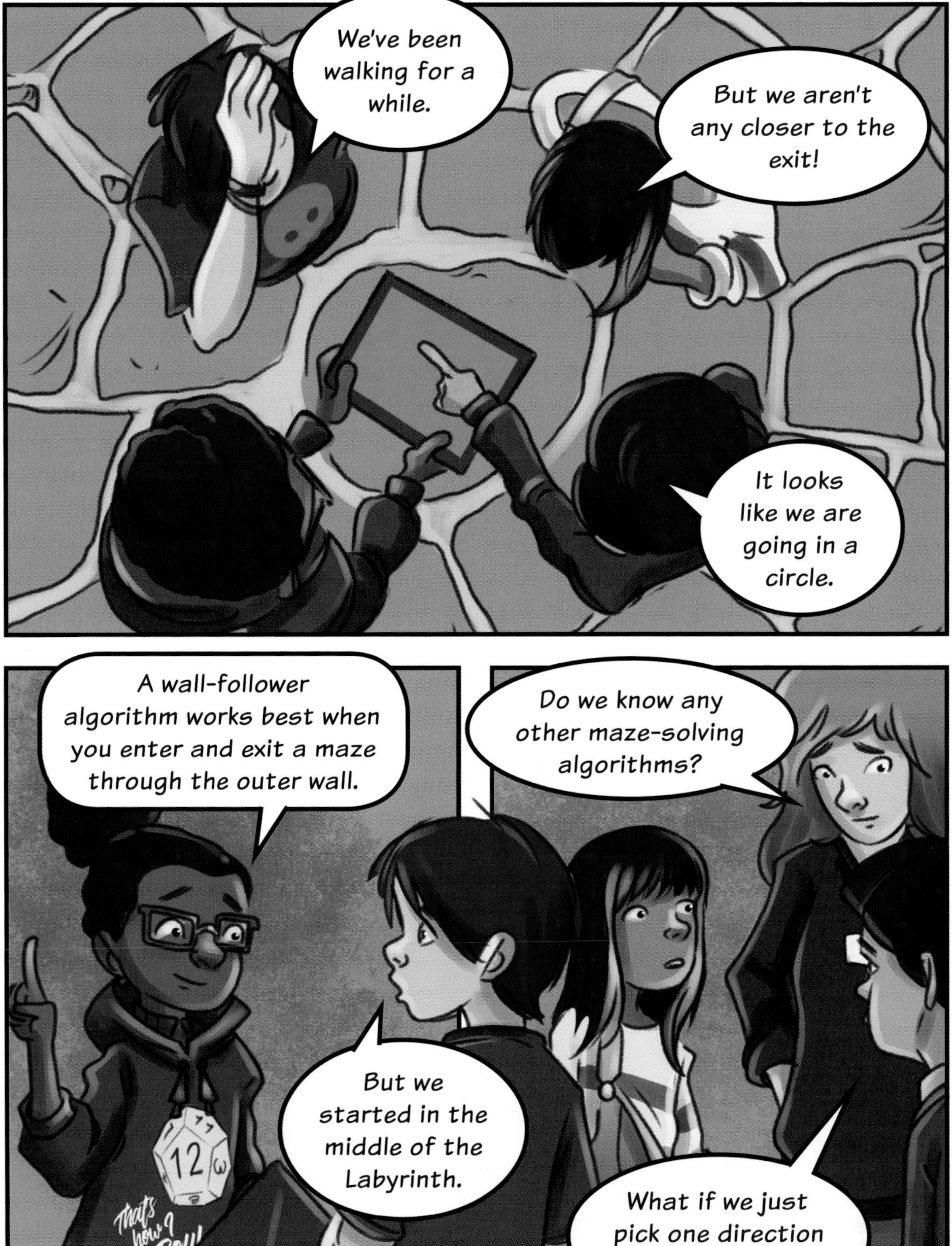
We've been walking for a while.
But we aren't any closer to the exit!
It looks like we are going in a circle.
A wall-follower algorithm works best when you enter and exit a maze through the outer wall.
Do we know any other maze-solving algorithms?
But we started in the middle of the Labyrinth.
What if we just pick one direction and go that way?

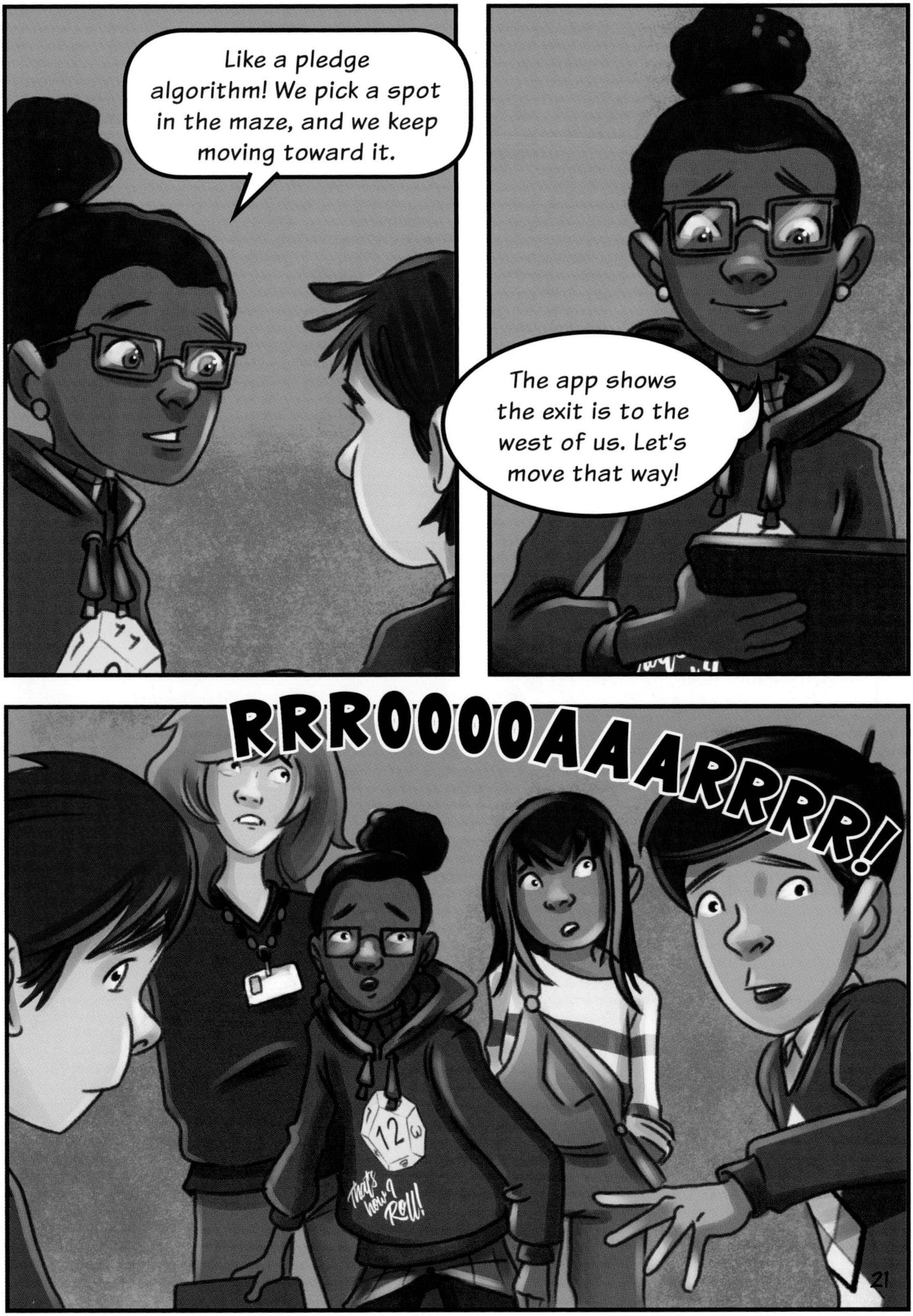

Like a pledge algorithm! We pick a spot in the maze, and we keep moving toward it.
The app shows the exit is to the west of us. Let's move that way!
RRROOOOAAARRRRR!
That's how I ROLL!

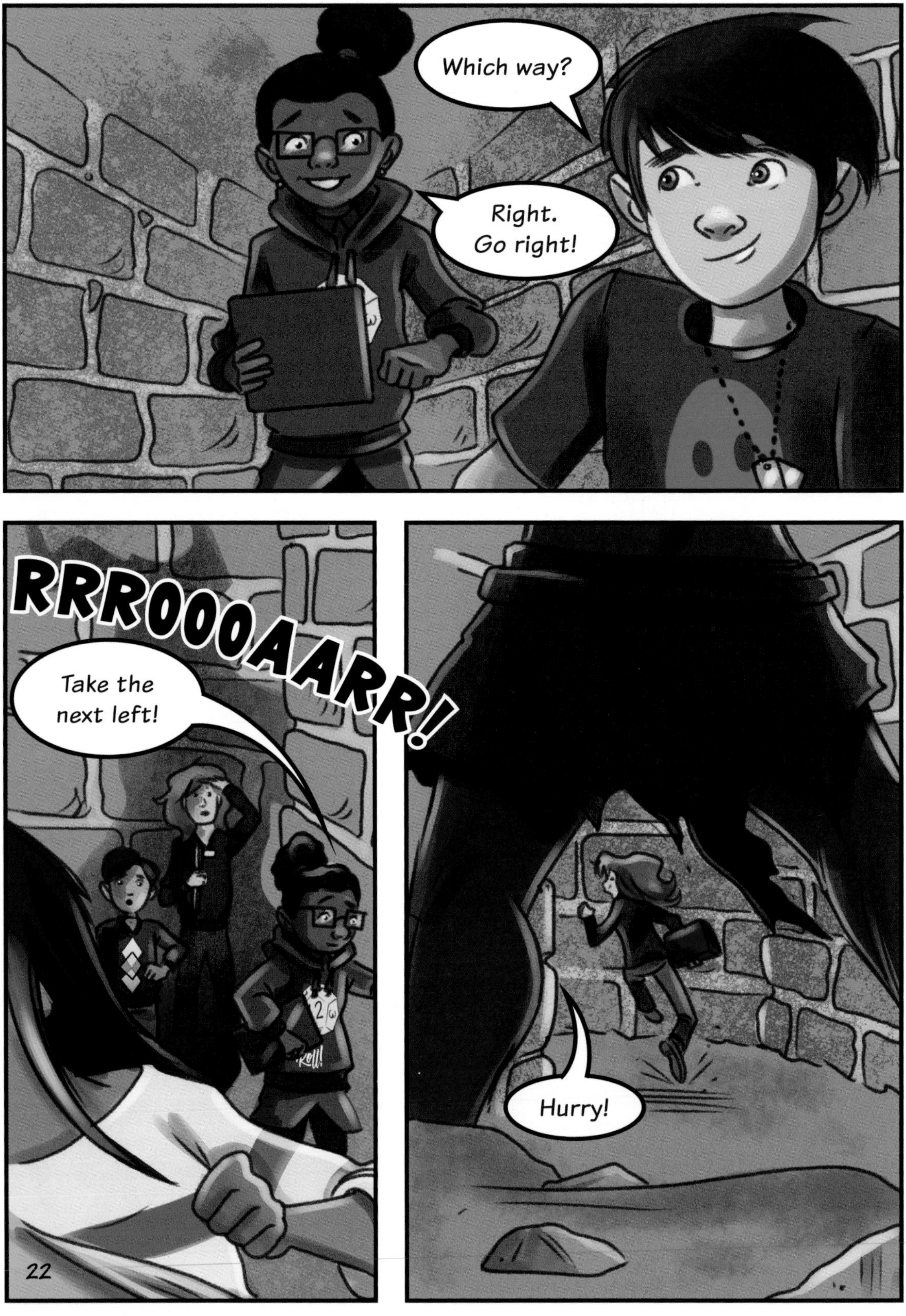
Which way?
Right. Go right!
RRROOOAARR!
Take the next left!
Hurry!

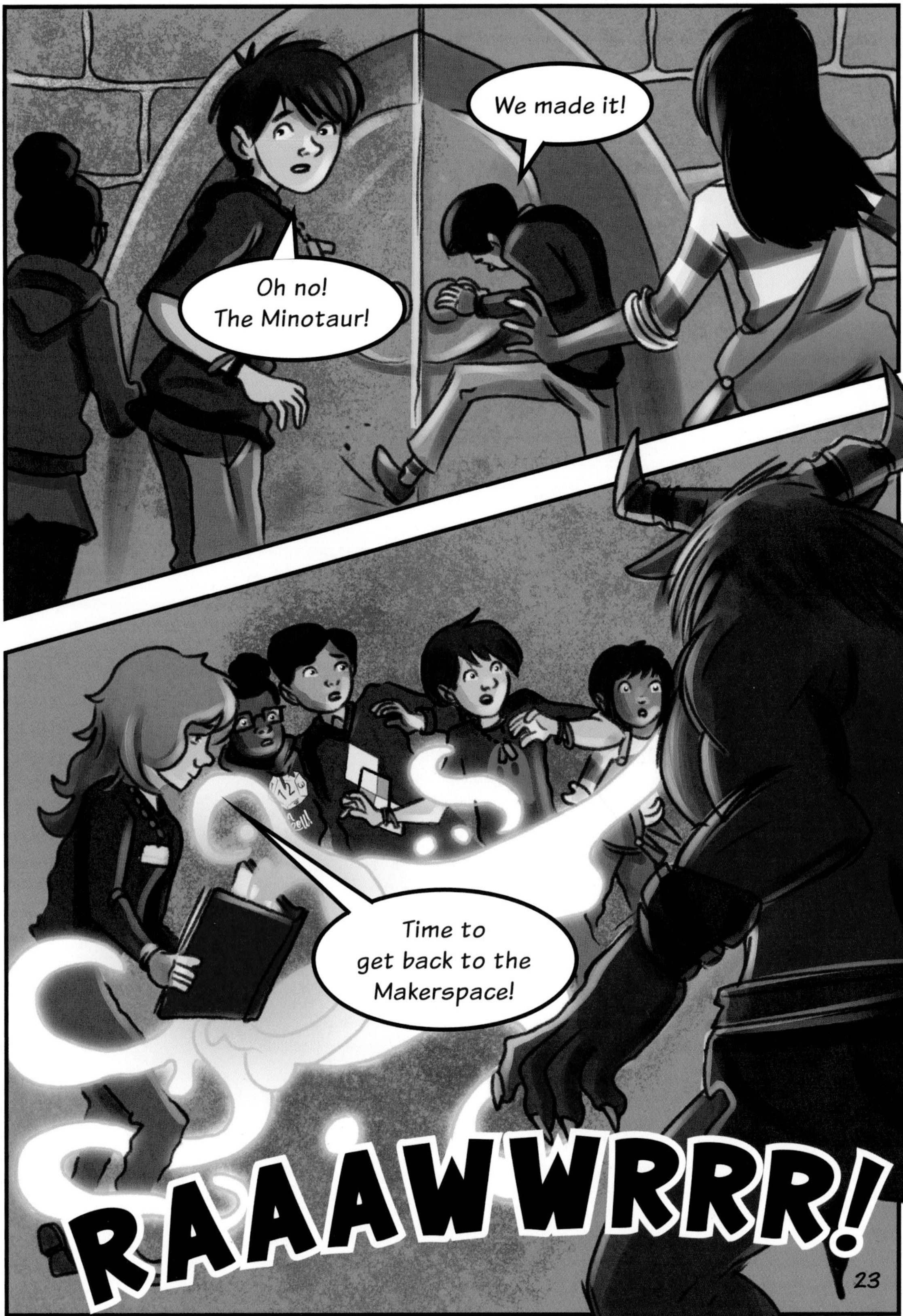
Oh no!
The Minotaur!
We made it!
Time to get back to the Makerspace!
RAAAWRRR!

ESCAPE FROM THE MAZE

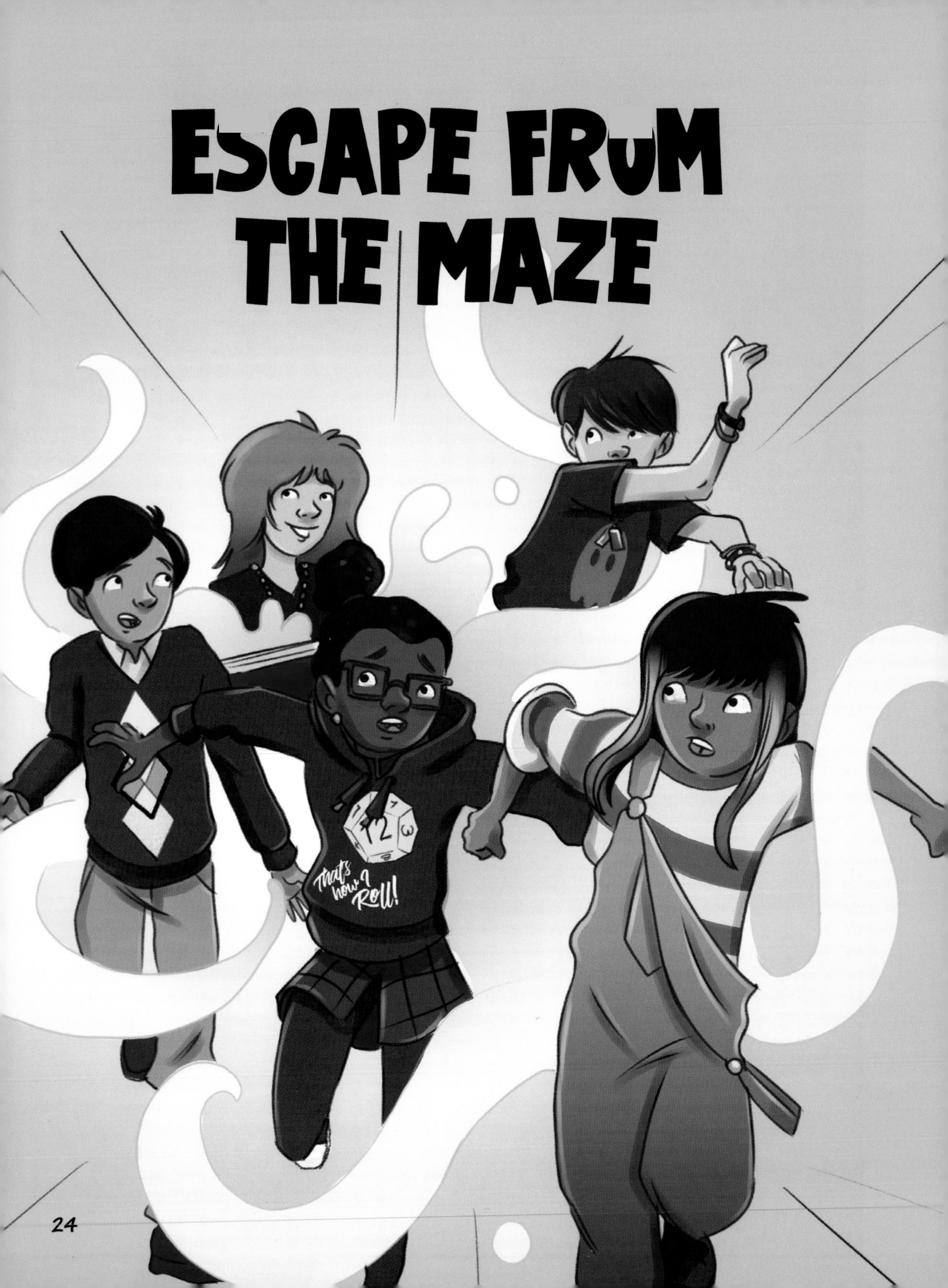
That's how I ROLL!

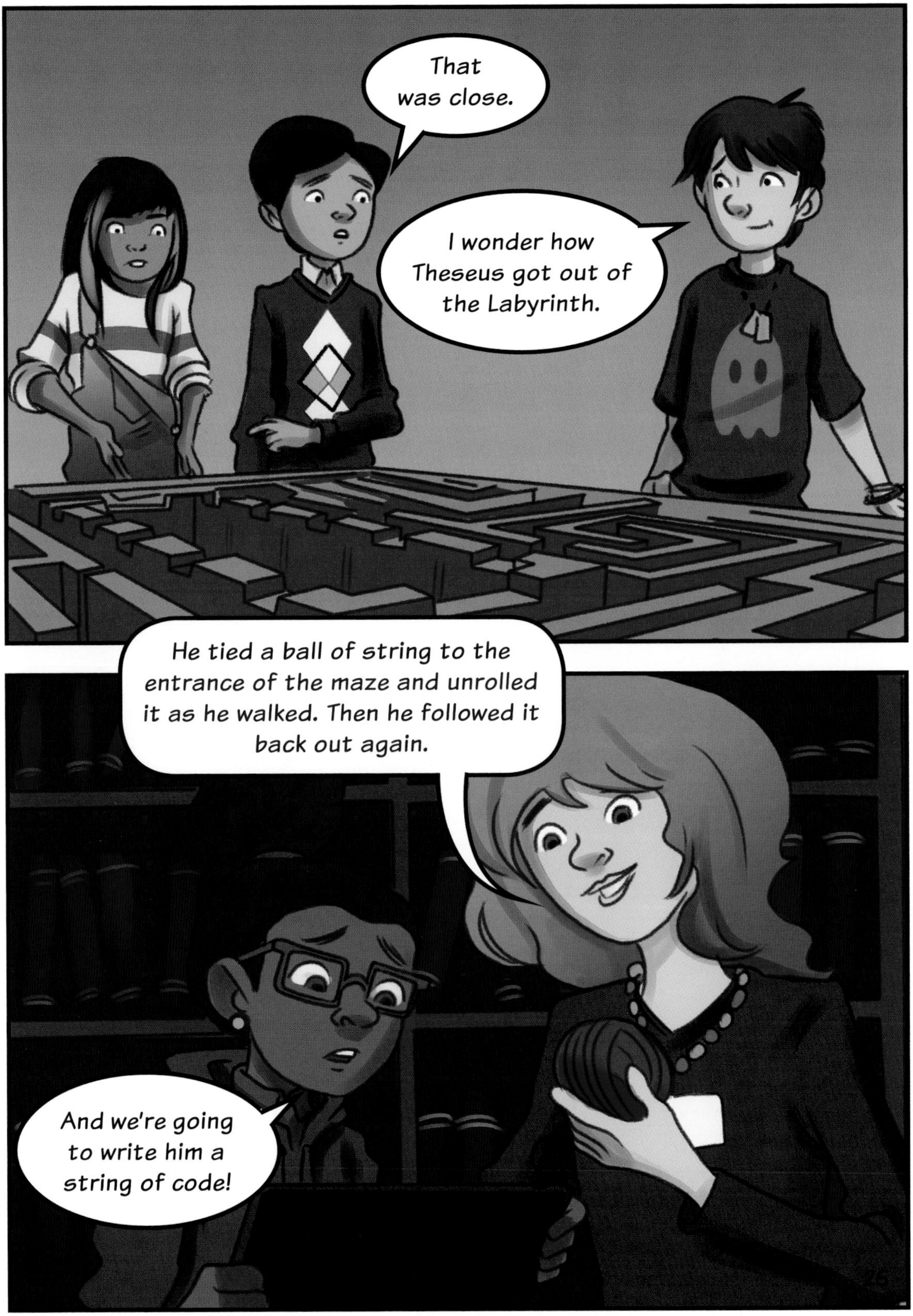
That was close.
I wonder how Theseus got out of the Labyrinth.
He tied a ball of string to the entrance of the maze and unrolled it as he walked. Then he followed it back out again.
And we're going to write him a string of code!

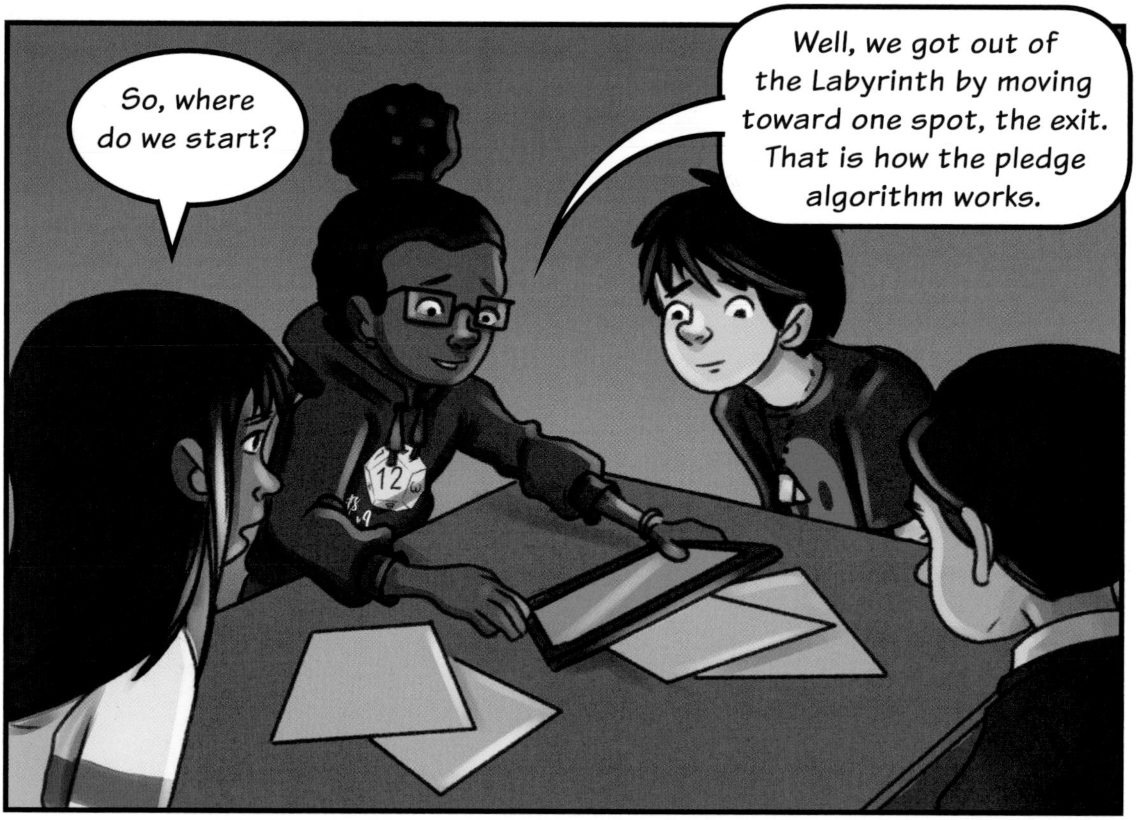
So, where do we start?
Well, we got out of the Labyrinth by moving toward one spot, the exit. That is how the pledge algorithm works.

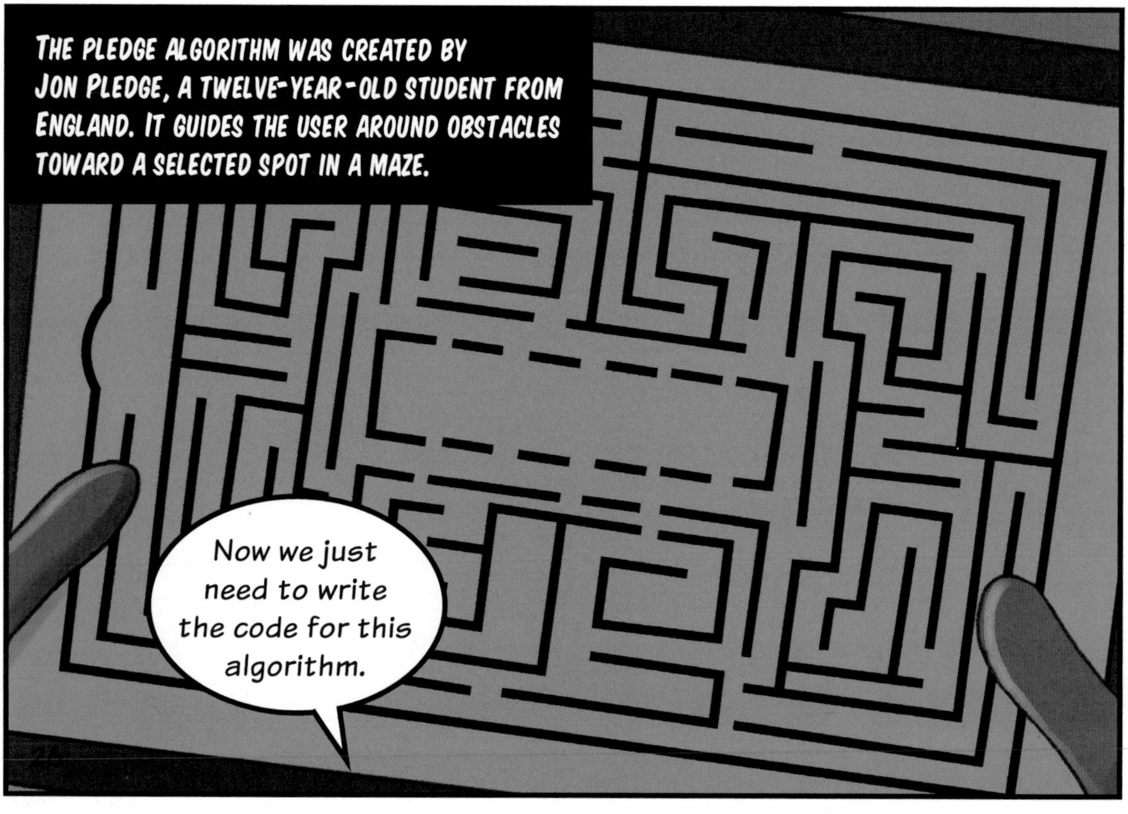
THE PLEDGE ALGORITHM WAS CREATED BY JON PLEDGE, A TWELVE-YEAR-OLD STUDENT FROM ENGLAND. IT GUIDES THE USER AROUND OBSTACLES TOWARD A SELECTED SPOT IN A MAZE.
Now we just need to write the code for this algorithm.

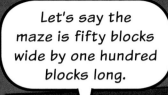

Let's say the maze is fifty blocks wide by one hundred blocks long.

We started in the center of the Labyrinth.

START LOCATION

X = 50

Y = 25

And the entrance is directly west of the lair.

START LOCATION

X = 50

Y = 25

END LOCATION

X = 0

Y = 25

Got it.

Now I need to set the color of the walls.

Anything else?

We just need to assign Theseus a color.

How about red?

WALL COLOR = BLACK

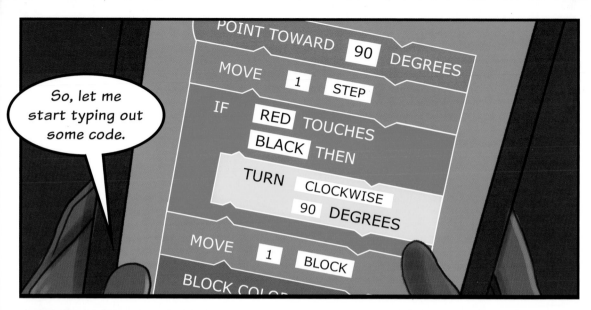

POINT TOWARD 90 DEGREES
MOVE 1 STEP
IF RED TOUCHES BLACK THEN
TURN CLOCKWISE 90 DEGREES
MOVE 1 BLOCK
So, let me start typing out some code.
THE STUDENTS SLOWLY WRITE A STRING OF CODE FOR THE PLEDGE ALGORITHM.
Let's test it out.
I think that's it!
We did it!

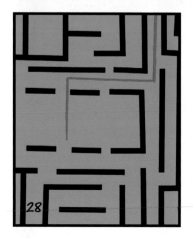

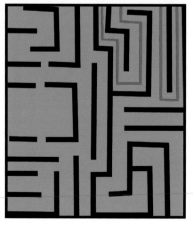

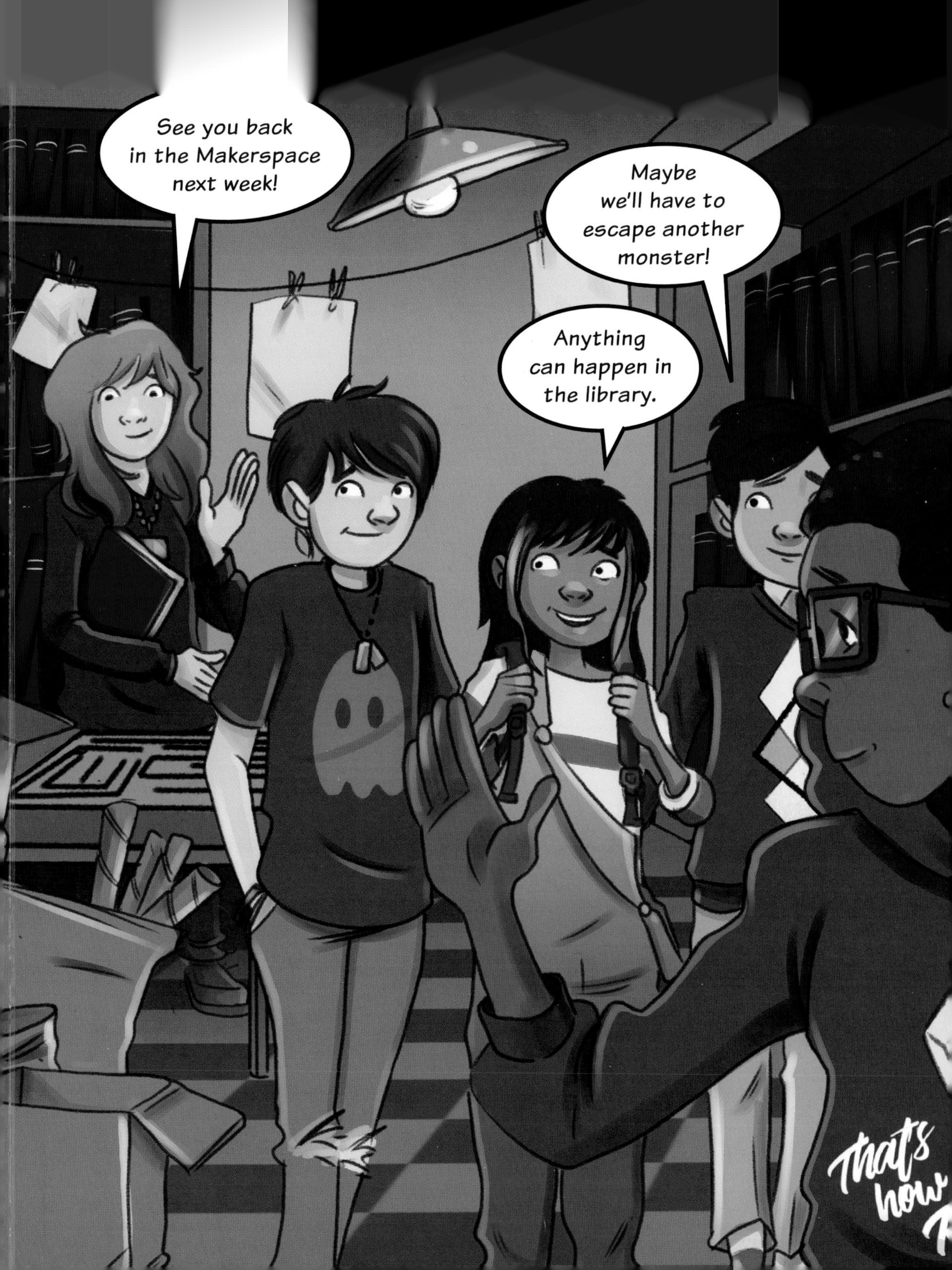
See you back in the Makerspace next week!
Maybe we'll have to escape another monster!
Anything can happen in the library.
That's
how

GLOSSARY

algorithm—set of step-by-step instructions that helps solve a problem or perform a task

code—series of symbols, numbers, and letters that instruct a computer to perform a certain function

diorama—miniature representation of a scene

Labyrinth—maze-like structure from the ancient Greek myth about Theseus and the Minotaur

lair—place where an animal lives

myth—made-up story about ancient history

CREATE YOUR OWN MAKERSPACE!

1. Find a place to store supplies. It could be a large area, like the space in this story. But it can also be a cart, bookshelf, or storage bin.

2. Make a list of supplies that you would like to have. Include items found in your recycling bin, such as cardboard boxes, tin cans, and plastic bottles (caps too!). Add art materials, household items such as rubber bands, paper clips, straws, and any other materials useful for planning, building, and creating.

3. Pass out your list to friends and parents. Ask them for help in gathering the materials.

4. It's time to create. Let your imagination run wild!

SOLVE A MAZE!

WHAT YOU NEED

- **1 six-sided die**
- **Theseus**
    (a toy figure to mark your
    place in the maze)
- **Paper and pencil**
- **A maze**

In this story, the students use different algorithms to try to get out of
the Labyrinth. Algorithms are important in coding. They tell a computer
how to solve a specific problem.

Test out two of Codie's algorithms to see which works best for your maze.

RANDOM MOUSE ALGORITHM
Randomly pick a direction to turn.

1. Place Theseus at the start of the maze.

2. Move him forward until he needs to decide
   which way to turn or runs into a wall.

3. Make a tally mark on your paper.

4. Roll the die. If it shows 1, 2, or 3, take the
   left path; if it shows 4, 5, or 6, take the
   right path. (If there are three possible
   directions, turn left on a roll of 1 or 2, go
   straight on a 3 or 4, and turn right on a
   5 or 6.)

5. Repeat steps two through four until you
   reach the end of the maze. If you have
   not reached the end after one hundred
   turns, stop.

WALL-FOLLOWER ALGORITHM
Follow the left wall through the maze.

1. Place Theseus at the start of the maze.

2. Move him forward until there is a left
   turn or he runs into a wall.

3. Make a tally mark on your paper.

4. Turn Theseus ninety degrees so that he
   always follows the wall on his left.

5. Repeat steps two through four until you
   reach the end of the maze. If you have
   not reached the end after one hundred
   turns, stop.

   Note: You can also try this algorithm
   using the right wall.

Compare the tally marks for each algorithm. Which one used the
fewest steps or got you farthest through the maze?

FURTHER RESOURCES

Harris, Patricia. *Gareth's Guide to Becoming a Rock Star Coder*. New York: Gareth Stevens, 2018.

Hoena, Blake. *Theseus and the Minotaur: A Graphic Retelling*. North Mankato, MN: Capstone, 2015.

Hubbard, Ben. *How Coding Works*. North Mankato, MN: Heinemann Raintree, 2017.

Miller, Shannon McClintock, and Blake Hoena. *A 3-D Printing Mission*. North Mankato, MN: Capstone, 2019.